Where's My Mommy?

By Carol Roth

Illustrated by Sean Julian

NorthSouth
New York / London

Little Kitty lived on a farm.

One day, after eating her lunch, she got very, very sleepy. She curled up in the barn to take a nice little nap.

While she was napping, her mommy went for a walk.

When Little Kitty woke up, her mommy wasn't there.

"Where's my mommy?" Little Kitty asked.

She wandered all around the barn. She couldn't find her mommy anywhere.

"I'd better go and find her," she said.

She slipped out through the barn door, but she didn't have any idea where to look.

She saw a little calf.

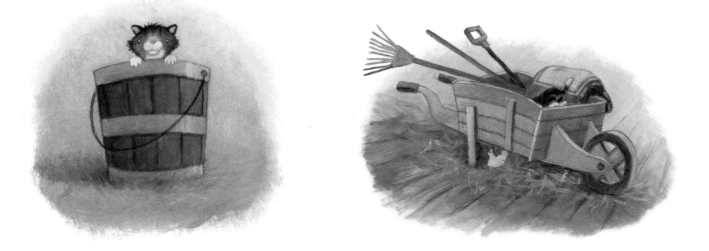

"Can you please help me?" asked Little Kitty. "I'm trying to find my mommy, but I don't know where she is."

The calf said,
"Listen to me carefully.
I'll tell you what to do.
Whenever I want my mommy,
I just call MOO, MOO, MOO."

So Little Kitty called, "MOO, MOO, MOO,"
but the mommy **COW** came running!
"That's not *my* mommy," said Little Kitty.
And she strolled along to ask somebody else.

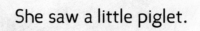

She saw a little piglet.

"Can you please help me?" asked Little Kitty.
"I'm looking for my mommy, but I don't know
where to find her."

The piglet said,
"I'm sure that I can help you.
I'll tell you what to say.
You simply call out OINK, OINK, OINK,
and Mommy comes right away!"

So Little Kitty called, "OINK, OINK, OINK,"
but the mommy **pig** came running!

"That's not *my* mommy," said Little Kitty.
And she wandered on some more.

She saw a little duckling.

"Can you please help me?" asked Little Kitty.
"My mommy is missing, and I need her to come back."

The duckling said,
"My mommy always told me
if I want her to come back,
stand up tall . . . open wide,
and call out QUACK, QUACK, QUACK."

So Little Kitty stood up tall . . . opened wide,
and called out, **"QUACK, QUACK, QUACK,"**
but the mommy **duck** came running!
"That's not *my* mommy," said Little Kitty.
And she wandered off again.

She saw a little colt.
"Can you please help me?"
asked Little Kitty. "I really
need to find my mommy."

The colt said,
"Silly Little Kitty,
I'll show you the way.
If you want your mommy,
just call NEIGH, NEIGH, NEIGH."

So Little Kitty called, "NEIGH, NEIGH, NEIGH,"
but the mommy **horse** came running!
"Where's MY mommy!" Little Kitty said.

Feeling very, very sad, she curled up in a little ball and
started to cry.

At first she cried softly . . . "Meow, meow, meow . . .
meow, meow, meow."

Then she cried a little louder . . . "Meow, meow,
meow . . . meow, meow, meow!"

Then she cried out very loud . . . "MEOW, MEOW,
MEOW! . . . MEOW, MEOW, MEOW!"

The mommy cat heard her and, quick as a wink, she came running.

"HERE'S my mommy!" said the happy Little Kitty.

"Yes, Mommy's here!" said the mommy cat as she licked her Little Kitty all over.

"I came running as soon as I heard your call."

Then the two of them walked back to the barn, so happy to be together once more.

Little Kitty never forgot how to call her mommy again.